10 3

Some words about Space:

"GRRRRRRRRR"
A black hole

"Ve vant vour vnowledge"
A Venutian

"Anyone seen my golf ball?"
An Apollo astronaut

"Three squeaks for Barry!"
The class hamsters

"right a squidge...left a squodge"
Daisy

**"WHAT ON EARTH
HAVE YOU DONE!!!"**
Daisy's mum

More Daisy adventures!

DAISY AND THE TROUBLE WITH LIFE

DAISY AND THE TROUBLE WITH NATURE

DAISY AND THE TROUBLE WITH ZOOS

DAISY AND THE TROUBLE WITH GIANTS

DAISY AND THE TROUBLE WITH KITTENS

DAISY AND THE TROUBLE WITH CHRISTMAS

DAISY AND THE TROUBLE WITH MAGGOTS

DAISY AND THE TROUBLE WITH COCONUTS

DAISY AND THE TROUBLE WITH BURGLARS

DAISY AND THE TROUBLE WITH SPORTS DAY

DAISY AND THE TROUBLE WITH PIGGY BANKS

DAISY AND THE TROUBLE WITH VAMPIRES

DAISY AND THE TROUBLE WITH CHOCOLATE

DAISY AND THE TROUBLE WITH SCHOOL TRIPS

DAISY AND THE TROUBLE WITH UNICORNS

DAISY AND THE TROUBLE WITH LONDON

JACK BEECHWHISTLE: ATTACK OF THE GIANT SLUGS

JACK BEECHWHISTLE: RISE OF THE HAIRY HORROR

Kes Gray

DAISY

and the trouble with

SPACE

PUFFIN

PUFFIN BOOKS

UK | USA | Canada | Ireland | Australia
India | New Zealand | South Africa

Puffin Books is part of the Penguin Random House group of companies
whose addresses can be found at global.penguinrandomhouse.com.

www.penguin.co.uk
www.puffin.co.uk
www.ladybird.co.uk

Penguin
Random House
UK

First published 2024

001

Text design by Kim Musselle
Printed in Great Britain by Clays Ltd, Elcograf S.p.A.

A CIP catalogue record for this book is available from the British Library
The authorized representative in the EEA is Penguin Random House Ireland,
Morrison Chambers, 32 Nassau Street, Dublin D02 YH68

ISBN: 978–0–2416–3202–4

All correspondence to
Red Fox, Penguin Random House Children's
One Embassy Gardens, New Union Square
5 Nine Elms Lane, London SW8 5DA

MIX
Paper from
responsible sources
FSC® C018179
www.fsc.org

Penguin Random House is committed to a
sustainable future for our business, our readers
and our planet. This book is made from Forest
Stewardship Council® certified paper.

To Natalie

CHAPTER 1

The trouble with space is it only comes

out at night! Which is all right if you're a grown-up; grown-ups are allowed to stay up as long as they want to, but I'm not. My mum makes me go to bed just as night-time is starting. Which would be fine if my bed was next to my bedroom window. If my bed was right beside my bedroom window, I could lie under my covers with my head on my pillow and see straight up into the sky.

But I can't. Because my bed is nowhere near my bedroom window. Which means when I look up, I can't see the Moon, I can't see the stars and I can't see the black bits around the edges. All I can see is boring old BEDROOM CEILING!

How am I possibly meant to solve the mysteries of the universe if I'm not allowed to even look up into space?! Solving the mysteries of the universe is absolutely impossible if you can't look up and see the Moon or the stars or the black bits in between.

It's EVEN HARDER if your mum forces you to go to bed before midnight AND draws your curtains when you go to bed too. WHICH ISN'T MY FAULT!

CHAPTER 2

It was just over a week ago that absolutely everyone in my class caught Space Fever. Don't worry, it's not a serious disease or anything; it's just something that makes you want to know more and more and more about the universe and beyond and beyond and beyond!

Guess how big the universe is?

MASSIVE!

Barry Morely told us just how massive in his special class talk two Fridays ago.

The trouble with special class talks

is you are only allowed to do them under special circumstances. Barry's circumstances were totally special, because guess what our head teacher, Mr Copford, let him do?

GO ON HOLIDAY IN ACTUAL TERM TIME!

Can you imagine how special that must feel, being allowed out of school while all your class friends are still totally in school, doing lessons and tests and homework and everything?

Mr Copford has never allowed me and my mum to go on holiday during term time, or Gabby and her parents. Even our teacher, Mrs Peters, hasn't been allowed to go on holiday during term time! But Barry Morely was totally allowed, because guess what type of holiday his parents had taken him on?

AN EDUCATIONAL ONE!

The trouble with educational holidays is at first they don't sound very

interesting. But when you find out that someone in your class has just been to an actual space station in actual Florida in the actual United States of actual America, and, not only that, gone for an actual ride in a space rocket right up into ACTUAL SPACE, it makes you nearly fall off your chair!

In fact, Jack Beechwhistle really did fall off his chair! Mind you, he's always doing that.

To make sure Mr Copford would definitely allow Barry to go, Barry's mum and dad had promised that he would do a special class talk when he came back to school. Lucky us! I couldn't wait to hear it, Gabby couldn't wait to hear it, everyone in our class couldn't wait to hear it, even our class hamsters couldn't wait to hear it!

And we didn't have long to wait either!

CHAPTER 3

On the very first morning of his very first day back at school, Barry stood up in front of the whole entire class and did his special talk. Luckily mine and Gabby's desk is right at the front, so we both had a really good view.

Barry didn't seem to be in the slightest bit nervous. He just walked to the front of the class, looked up and then pointed at the ceiling.

"Space," said Barry. "The universe . . ." said Barry. "What mysteries do they hold? There is only one way to find out."

"Go on holiday during term time," whispered Gabby.

"Space travel," said Barry. "The more Man journeys into space . . ."

"And women," said Vicky Carrow, putting her hand up.

"Yes, sorry," said Barry. "The more Man and women journey into space, the more the Unknown will become Known."

"*Men* and women, not man and women," said Daniel Carrington.

"Let Barry speak, please, Class," said Mrs Peters. "He has many interesting and exciting things to tell us about. Please continue, Barry. You're doing very well."

Mrs Peters was right. Barry was doing better than very well – he had so many interesting and exciting things to say it made our brains boggle!

Did you know that the universe is made up of two different bits?

Barry calls one bit the Knowniverse, because it's the bit of the universe that scientists know about. The other bit is the Unknowniverse, because it is the bit of the universe scientists don't know about, because telescopes aren't good enough to see that far.

That's **the trouble with telescopes**. They need to get their act together.

Plus did you know that space and the universe aren't the same thing?

The universe is all the planets and stars and other starry-type objects that are happening up in space. And space is all the black bits in between!

How amazing is that?! Me and Gabby thought space and the universe were two different words for exactly the same thing. But they're not. They are only kind of the same thing. Which is quite boggly.

But then Barry got even bogglier. Because guess how big the universe is?

It's TOTALLY WHOPPING!

Guess how far my classroom is from the Moon?

THREE HUNDRED AND EIGHTY-FOUR THOUSAND, FOUR HUNDRED BLOOMIN' KILOMETRES!!!

Guess how far my classroom is from the Sun?

ONE HUNDRED AND FORTY-NINE MILLION BLOOMIN' KILOMETRES!!!!!!

Guess how far my classroom is from the furthest-most edge of the Knowniverse?

FORTY-SIX AND A HALF BILLION BLINKING LIGHT YEARS!!!!!!!! (Minus one metre if you stood on my desk.)

(Light years are like space kilometres by the way. Only much, much longer.)

Now, guess what . . . Guess how far my classroom is from the very, very, very end of the Unknowniverse?

NO ONE HAS THE SLIGHTEST, SLIGHTEST, SLIGHTEST IDEA!!!!!!!!!!!!!!!! Because until telescopes learn to see a whole lot further, it's going to be one whopping great space mystery that no one can ever solve!!!!!!!!!!!!!!!!!!!!!!!!!!!!!!!!!

Barry says the mysteries of the universe have puzzled people since the invention of people. Cavemen used to get puzzled by it, Romans used to get puzzled by it,  Henry the Eighth probably got puzzled by it, even Luke Skywalker is probably puzzled by it, and he actually lives in actual space!

What I can tell you for sure is that if your school gave you a space address it would be this:

Your chair
Your classroom
Your school
Your town
Your city
Your country
Your continent
Your planet
Your galaxy (I'll tell you all about galaxies later)
The Knowniverse
The Unknowniverse

16

And beyond
And beyond and beyond!
Because some scientists think that the whole entire universe just goes on and on forever! And ever and ever and ever!!! How boggly, boggly, boggly is that?!!!

When the school bell rang for morning break it sooooooo made everyone jump.

That's **the trouble with your mind being boggled**. It makes it difficult for your brain to keep up.

"Thank you very much indeed, Barry, for the first half of a very enlightening talk," said Mrs Peters.

"First half?" I gasped.

"FIRST HALF????" EVERYONE GASPED!

That's right: we thought Barry's talk was over, but it had only just begun!

"Where will you be taking us after breaktime, Barry?" said Mrs Peters.

"On a mission to Mars," he said!

CHAPTER 4

You should have seen how popular Barry was during morning break! I've never seen the quiet bench so busy. Or noisy!!

Everyone wanted to ask Barry questions about space, like, "Is the Moon really made out of cheese?" and, "Why is Mars named after a chocolate bar?"

I think Barry was a bit boggled himself by all the questions he was being asked to answer. I'm not sure he knew which way to turn first!

"Give him some space!" said Collette Simpson, trying to give Barry room to breathe.

Trouble is, everyone thought she was joking, so instead of moving away from the quiet bench, everyone tried to get on it and ask him another space question!

Guess how many children were sitting next to Barry before Miss Leames came over to tell them off?

SEVENTEEN!

The quiet bench only has room for five bottoms!

Luckily, the school bell rang again before it could break under the weight!

And before Barry could get totally, totally squashed!!!

Luckily, by the time we had walked across the playground and got back to our classroom, Barry had managed to get his breath completely back. And he'd managed to comb his hair. (It got a bit ruffled on the quiet bench!)

"Welcome back, children," said Mrs Peters. "Will you please give another big round of applause to Barry? I'm sure the second half of his talk will be out of this world!!"

Everyone gave Barry the biggest claps they could clap and then kept on clapping until Mrs Peters did her 'silence is golden' action.

"Thank you, children," said Mrs Peters. "Barry, the class is all yours."

As soon as Barry got to the front of the class, he did his 'pointing at the ceiling' action again.

"Mars . . ." said Barry. "The Red Planet," said Barry. "Is there life on Mars? Was there life on Mars? What mysteries does the Red Planet hold? There is only one way to find out."

"Go on holiday during term time," whispered Gabby AGAIN.

"A journey into space," said Barry, "in a rocket-fuelled space shuttle to . . ."

we all cheered!

CHAPTER 5

Barry's mission to Mars was the most exciting thing I have ever, ever, ever heard in my whole entire life!

It was like something out of a movie! It was like something you read in a space comic! There was action, there was danger, there were even some birds that nearly got burned to a crisp! Even when I think about it now it still gives me the shivers.

It even gives my shivers the shivers!!!!!!

This is how it went!

ACTUAL SPACE STATION IN ACTUAL FLORIDA:
BRAVE CHILDREN FROM ALL OVER THE WORLD GATHER, HOPING TO BE CHOSEN FOR AN IMPORTANT MISSION TO MARS.

THREE CHILDREN ARE CAREFULLY SELECTED. AMONG THEM IS A BOY FROM ENGLAND.

HIS NAME?

BARRY MORELY.

MISSION BRIEFING ROOM:

THE FEARLESS CHILDREN GATHER FOR THEIR PRE-FLIGHT BRIEFING.

Welcome, Space Crew. The mission you are about to undertake is the bravest in the history of mankind. You will need to be brave and alert, and work as a team.

You will be driving a super-fast, hydrogen-powered, totally awesome spacecraft. So, seatbelts at the ready!

Your mission to Mars is going to be dark, bumpy, spinny and space-sicky. But don't worry – we will put you into hypersleep for six months and wake you up for space breakfast when you get there.

HYPERSLEEP!!!!?

Yes, hypersleep: a journey of six months will only feel like six seconds.

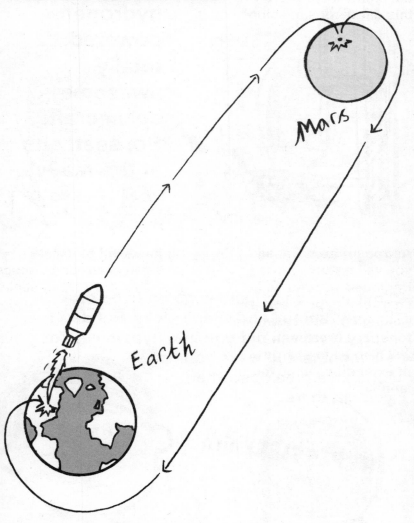

TEAM BRIEFING:

Astronaut Morely, you will be Mission Commander. You will be responsible for the safety of your crew on this dangerous mission.

Astronaut from Peru, you will be Mission Pilot. You will steer the spacecraft down to the rocky surface of Mars.

Astronaut from Canada, you will be Mission Engineer. You will be in charge of hypersleep and waking up your crewmates for space breakfast. You will also be in charge of extending wings for landing.

In the event of a Mars Mission emergency, space buttons and control sticks will be provided.

BRIEFING COMPLETE.

THE SPACE CREW ENTER THEIR CAPSULE AND TAKE THEIR FLIGHT POSITIONS IN THE COCKPIT.

ASTRONAUT MORELY PULLS DOWN HIS SPECIAL SPACE-SAFETY RESTRAINT AND RESTS THE BACK OF HIS HEAD FIRMLY AGAINST THE HEADREST.

THE REST OF THE CREW FOLLOW MORELY'S LEAD.

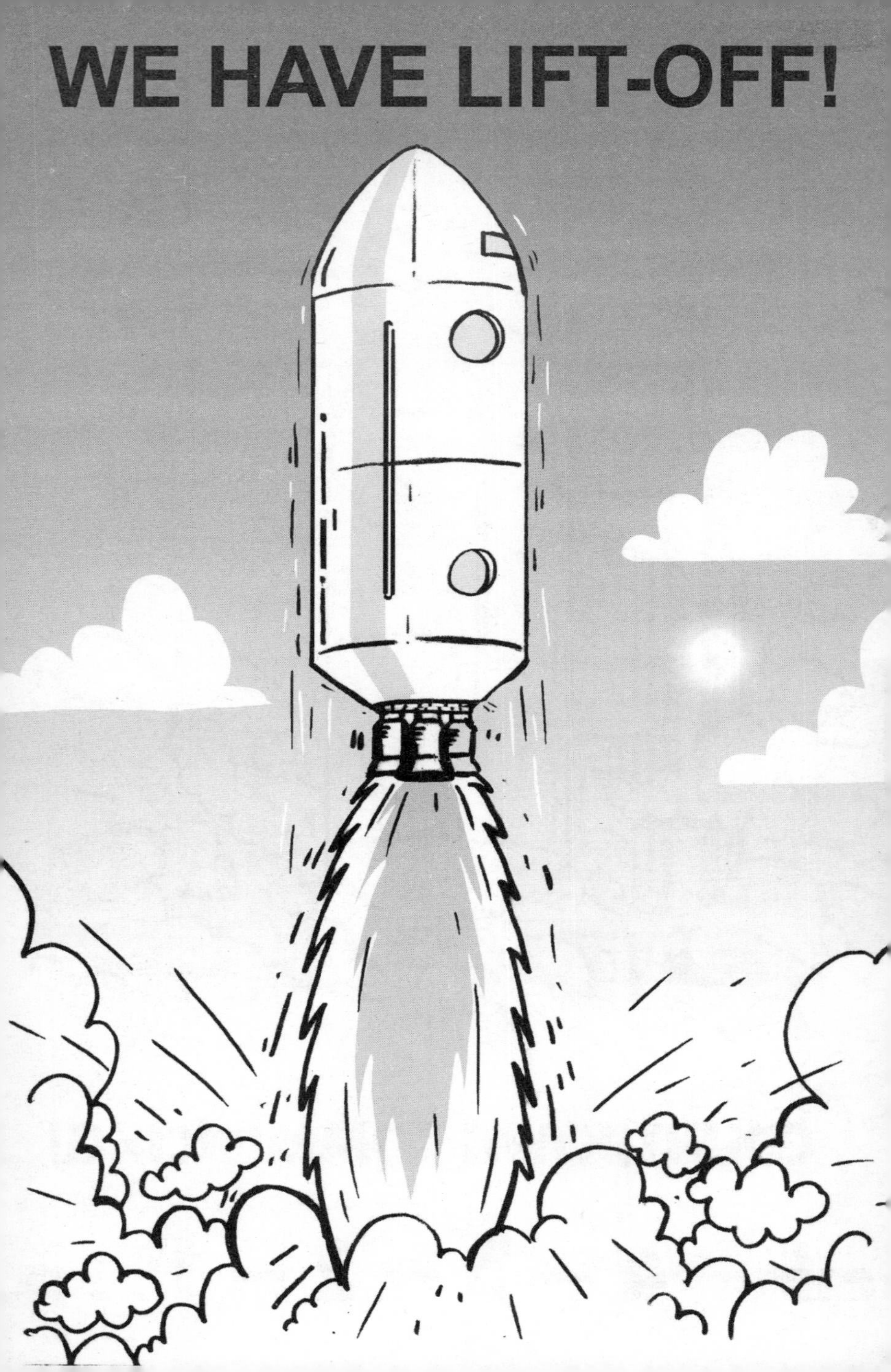
WE HAVE LIFT-OFF!

CLOUDS OF HOT SMOKE
BILLOW FROM THE GROUND.

BIRDS IN THE SKY
NEARLY GET FRAZZLED.

MISSION CONTROL:

**THE TOWER IS CLEAR.
YOUR JOURNEY
TO MARS IS
GO!!!!!**

THE SKY TURNS FROM CLOUDY TO BLUE.

THE BLUE TURNS TO DARK BLUE WITH FEWER CLOUDS.

THE DARK BLUE TURNS TO DARKER BLUE WITH STARS.

THE STARS TURN TO MORE STARS. LITTLE STARS AND BIG STARS. WHITE STARS AND BLUE STARS.

ZERO GRAVITY CONFIRMED!

Mission Pilot, keep the spacecraft steady!

NOW ORBITING THE EARTH! SPEED: 15,000 MILES PER HOUR!

SPACE STATION IN VIEW! WITH MOON BEHIND!

Mission Commander, check your crew are strapped in tight – activate hypersleep!

SIX SECONDS LATER:

WAKEY-WAKEY, TEAM! MARS APPROACHING.

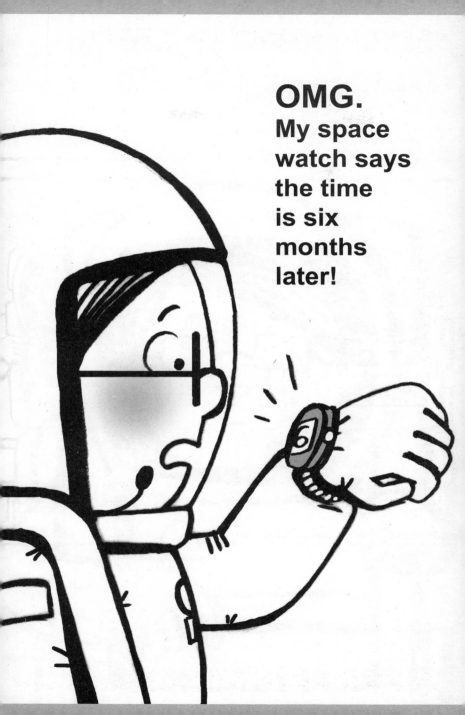

CREW ENGINEER, EXTEND WINGS FOR LANDING.

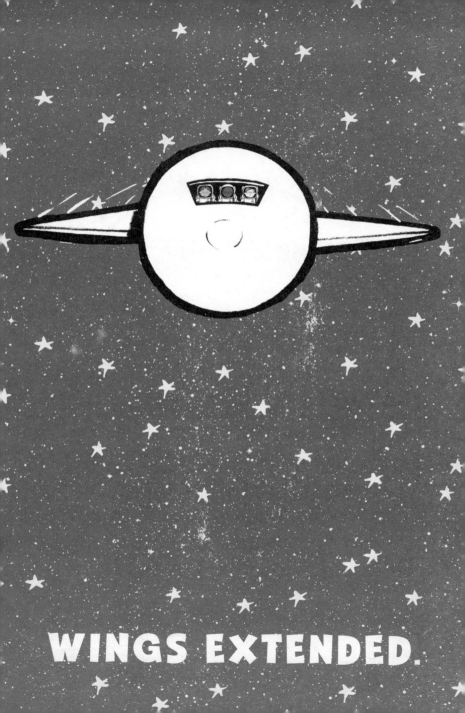

WINGS EXTENDED.

WHITEOUT ON RED PLANET!

REPEAT. WHITEOUT ON RED PLANET!

SNOWFLAKES OF DOOM!

ICICLES OF TERROR!

SNOW AND ICE APPROACHING!

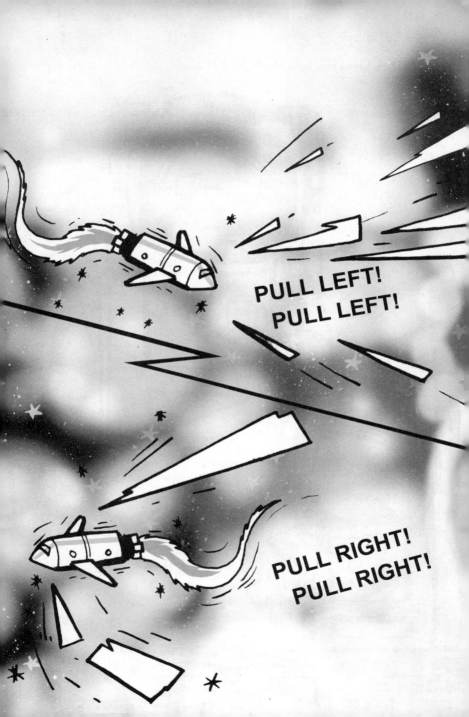

SAY YOUR PRAYERS, TEAM!

LANDING STRIP BURIED!

SPACE CANYON LOOMING!

DON'T MOVE A MUSCLE,

TEAM. IT'S MORELY TIME!

GOOD WORK, MORELY!

GOOD WORK, MARS MISSION TEAM!

"And that was my trip to Mars!" said Barry.

CHAPTER 6

As soon as Barry had finished his talk, EVERYONE in my class put their hand up. In fact, they put both hands up because there were so many more questions people wanted to ask him!

Luckily, I was right at the front, so Mrs Peters chose me first!

"Did any of the birds get frazzled by the flames coming out of your rocket?" I asked.

"What birds?" said Barry.

"When you took off in your rocket, you said you could see lots of birds in the sky above you, trying to get out of the way of your rocket. Did any of the birds get actually frazzled by your rocket?" I asked.

"I didn't see any get frazzled," said Barry.

"What about getting flame-grilled?" laughed Jack Beechwhistle.

"NEXT question," said Mrs Peters.

"Is Mars really red?" asked Bernadette Laine.

"I think so," said Barry. "But the snow blizzard made it look white when we got there."

"How did you manage to get back to Earth without moving a muscle?" asked Paula Potts.

"It wasn't a real space journey," said Barry. "It was a simulated one. When the lights came on at the end, my mission was over, so I could move all the muscles I wanted."

"What does 'simulated' mean?" asked Paula AGAIN, which was a bit naughty really, because we were only meant to ask one question each.

"A journey into space that is simulated," said Mrs Peters, "is a journey into space that isn't real but feels VERY, VERY, VERY real."

"So you didn't actually go to Mars?" said Paula.

"No," said Barry, "my mission to Mars was a theme-park ride that anyone can go on. You just have to queue up and wait your turn."

"I knew that," whispered Gabby.

"Me too," I whispered back.

Nobody cared anyway, because the questions just kept coming and coming and coming!

"What's zero gravity?" (Liam Chaldecott)

"Are meteors made of meat?" (Daniel McNicholl)

"Is the opposite of hydrogen 'lowdrogen'?" (Lottie Taylor)

"If you were sick in space, would your sick float around?" (Colin Kettle)

"Do space stations have tellies?" (Laura Donnelly)

"Do space stations have skate parks?" (Daniel Carrington)

"Do space stations have Wi-Fi?" (Lily Hanrahan)

"Do space stations have Coco Pops?" (Melanie Simpson)

"Did it hurt when they put you into hypersleep?" (Oliver Cornwall)

"When you almost crash-landed, did you think you were going to die?" (David Alexander)

"If you had died, would it have taken you less time to get to heaven? Because you were already much higher up than if you'd died on Earth?" (Stephanie Brakespeare)

Poor old Barry. I think he was really glad when it got to lunchtime.

"I think Mission Commander Morely has answered enough questions now, children," said Mrs Peters, clapping her hands really loudly.

"OHHHHHHHHHHHHHHHHHHHHH," said all the children who hadn't got to ask one. Including Gabby.

"The dinner bell is about to ring," said Mrs Peters, "so let's finish the morning with another big Class 5C round of applause for Barry. Our man on a mission!"

Everyone clapped so loudly I could barely hear the dinner bell when it rang.

"I'm eating my lunch on the quiet bench!" said Gabby.

"Me too," I said.

EVERYONE was going to eat their lunch on the quiet bench!

Until they realized Barry was eating his in the dinner hall!

CHAPTER 7

After lunch, everyone rocketed back to class. When we got there, we found that Mrs Peters had caught Space Fever too!

"Children," she said, "Barry's journey to Mars has certainly fired my imagination, and I can see it has clearly fired yours too! I have been thinking about all the questions that you asked Barry after his talk, and all the many questions that some of you didn't have time to ask."

"My question was going to be brilliant," whispered Gabby.

"Thank you, Gabriella." Mrs Peters frowned, before going back to smiling. "As I am sure you have learned, space is a topic that is far too big to squeeze into just one day at school, so for this reason I have decided to make the whole of next week 'SPACE WEEK'!"

"SPACE WEEK???!" everyone gasped.

"All day, every day," smiled Mrs Peters.

"ALL DAY, EVERY DAY!!!?" everyone gasped.

"Will we still have to do maths?" asked Jack Beechwhistle.

"Will we still have to do literacy?" asked Dottie Taylor.

"Next week, the only thing I will be asking you to think about is SPACE," smiled Mrs Peters.

As soon as we realized that we wouldn't be doing any normal lessons for ONE WHOLE ACTUAL WEEK, the whole of my class got really, really excited. Jack Beechwhistle fell off his chair again, Laura Donnelly tried to kiss the hamsters, Stephanie Brakespeare stood up and started flossing, and Paula Potts had to go to the loo!

It was the best Friday at school EVER!

"Space will be your special topic of study at school from this Friday all the way through to next Friday," smiled Mrs Peters. "Each day next week, I will be asking groups of you to share your very own space findings with the class. You will work together, learn together and present together, but before you do so I need to divide you up into teams."

"TEAMS!!!!?" everyone gasped.

The trouble with teams is as soon as we heard the word "TEAMS", everyone started thinking about who they wanted to be in a team with.

But it didn't matter, because Mrs Peters had already decided. She had written them down on a piece of paper during the lunch break. In fact, in the space of just one lunchtime Mrs Peters had got the whole of Space Week completely figured out.

First she told us who the teams would be.

"The teams for next week's Space Week will be:

TEAM SUN: Laura, Liam, Melanie, Bernadette and Daniel C.

TEAM MOON: Nishta, Harry, Vicky, Colin and Daniel M.

TEAM STARS: Daisy, Gabby, Oliver, Sanjay and Paula.

TEAM GRAVITY: Barry, Chelsea, Collette, Richard and Stephanie.

TEAM PLANETS: Lily, Jack, Lottie, Dottie and David."

Then she told us when each team would have to do their talks:

"On Monday afternoon, **Team Sun** will tell the class everything they have learned about the Sun," said Mrs Peters.

"MONDAYYYYY!!!!" gasped Team Sun.

(Poor old Team Sun. They only had the weekend and Monday morning to get their talk ready!)

Then on Tuesday afternoon, **Team Moon** would be telling the class everything they had learned about the Moon.

On Wednesday afternoon, my team would be telling the whole class about stars!

On Thursday afternoon, **Team Gravity** (mostly Barry) would be trying to explain how gravity works. (Or doesn't work.)

And on the last day of Space Week, **Team Planets** would be telling the class everything they had discovered about . . . you've guessed it, planets!

How cosmic is that?!

It was actually a really, really good job that Mrs Peters had decided who the teams for Space Week were going to be, because the children she had chosen for each team were only sitting one desk away from each other. So working as a team was really easy.

Within just seconds of finding out who our team was going to be, Gabby and me had turned our chairs round to talk to Oliver, Sanjay and Paula. Within minutes, the whole class had divided up into their teams too!

"I'll go to the library at the weekend and ask if they've got any books about stars!" said Sanjay.

"I'll research stars on my mum and dad's computer!" said Gabby.

"I'll look stars up on my laptop!" said Paula.

"I'll look stars up on my phone!" said Oliver.

"I'll look out of my bedroom window!" I told them.

For the rest of that Friday afternoon, all we thought about and talked about was stars. Not maths or literacy or spellings or history or anything normal at all, just STARS!

On our way home after school, Gabby invited me to go round to her house on Saturday.

"We can look up loads of stuff about stars on my mum and dad's computer together!" she said. "We can learn everything about stars there is to know!"

"What time can I come round?" I asked.

"I'm going shopping with my mum in the morning," said Gabby, "so come round to mine about eleven."

"Will do," I said, waving goodbye at the top of her road. "Oh, and by the way," I shouted, "what was that question you never had a chance to ask Barry?"

"What time do astronauts like to eat?" said Gabby.

"I don't know." I frowned. "What time *do* astronauts like to eat?"

"Launchtime!!" she giggled.

At first, I wasn't sure why she was laughing. Then I realized what she had done. It was a SPACE JOKE! I never knew there were jokes about space!

As soon as I got home, I told my mum Gabby's space joke and then all about Barry's simulated journey to Mars.

"Hypersleep!" she gasped. "Ooohhh, I love the sound of hypersleep. Just imagine what I could do if your bedroom had a hypersleep button, Daisy. Just think: I could switch you on and off with a flick of a switch! Oohhh yes, hypersleep sounds like every parent's dream!"

Thennnnnnnnnnnnnnnnn, once she'd fiiiiiiiiiiiiiiiiiiiiiiiiiiiiinally stopped talking about hypersleep, I asked her if I could move my bed next to my bedroom window.

And have my curtains taken down.

And change my bedtime to midnight.

I've already told you what her answer was.

"But I need to look at the stars!" I groaned.

"Bedrooms are for sleeping in, not stargazing in!" she said. "You can look at the stars until it's your bedtime, but after that I want your bedroom curtains and your eyelids firmly closed!"

"Right, that's it!" I said, stomping straight upstairs to put my pyjamas and dressing gown on.

"AND DON'T STOMP!"

my mum shouted. **"YOU'LL SHAKE THE HOUSE DOWN!"**

When I came back down the stairs, my mum nearly fainted on the spot.

"Daisy, it's quarter past four in the afternoon! The stars don't come out until seven!"

"Yes," I said, "and I'm not going to miss a single one!"

CHAPTER 8

The trouble with clouds is they totally, totally, totally ruin EVERYTHING!

At least they do if you're trying to do stargazing. Even if there were any stars in the sky that evening, I still didn't have ANY chance of gazing at them, because guess what . . .? From the second I ran up to my bedroom and looked out of my window, ALL I COULD SEE WAS CLOUD! In fact, the cloud was so thick, I couldn't even work out where the Moon was!!!!!

Then, when it came to bedtime, I didn't even have clouds to look at! All I had was bedroom ceiling!!!!!!!

The trouble with bedroom ceilings is they are the most boring things on Earth. In the universe, probably. They don't "twinkle, twinkle"; they don't make you think "how I wonder what you are". They just make you feel really, really, really bored until eventually your eyeballs either fall out or just give up and go to sleep.

Even when my eyeballs opened on Saturday morning, my bedroom ceiling was still there right above me, being the most boring thing on Earth.

Luckily, luckily, luckily, though, all that was about to change when I went to Gabby's!

The trouble with going to Gabby's is my mum always takes me in her car. Which is really nice of her, but she always does cleaning on Saturday mornings. And afternoons if I've been really messy. Not just cleaning either – sometimes she does washing and ironing too.

Which meant I didn't get round to Gabby's till TWO MINUTES past eleven. I'd have been even later if I hadn't got my pad and pencil case ready all by myself.

"Come and see what my mum has bought me!" said Gabby, grabbing me by the hand as soon as her front door opened and dragging me straight up the stairs to her bedroom.

Her very, very DARK bedroom.

"Why are your curtains still drawn?" I asked.

"LOOK UP!" she said.

When I looked up, my eyeballs nearly popped out! Because guess what Gabby had on her ceiling?

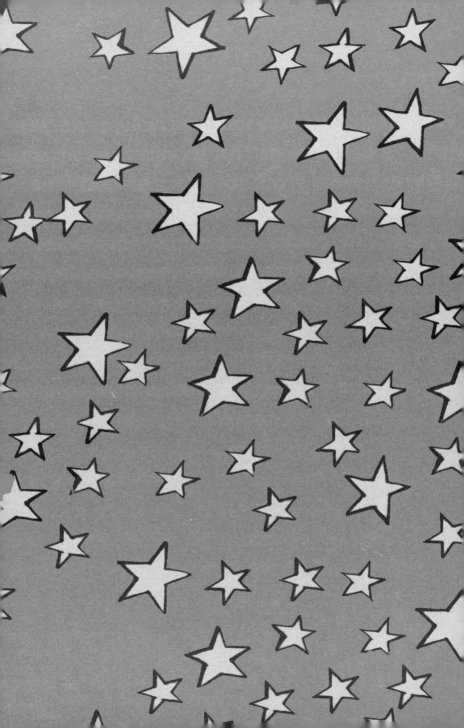

"They're glow-in-the-dark stars!" said Gabby. "You can stick them to your ceiling and look up at them when you're in bed! Aren't they brilliant?"

Gabby's glow-in-the-dark stars weren't just brilliant – they were hyperbrilliant!!!

"Come and see properly," she said, pulling me over to her bed and getting me to lie down right beside her.

"There's hundreds!" I gasped.

"Four packets!" Gabby said. "My mum only wanted to buy me three, but I told her three wouldn't be enough!"

"How do you get them to glow?" I asked.

"With a torch!" said Gabby. "You shine a torch on them, close your curtains and BINGO! Let there be stars!"

"I love them!" I said.

"I knew you would," said Gabby, pressing a surprise present into the palm of my hand. "That's why I've saved two for you!"

When I opened my fingers and saw two glow-in-the-dark stars glowing straight back at me, I nearly fainted!

"Thank you, thank you, thank you!!!"
I said, giving both of my glow-in-the-dark stars an even closer look.

"One can remind you of me." Gabby smiled. "And the other one can remind you of you!"

"How do you get them to stick?" I asked.

"You peel off the paper on the back of them!" she said.

"How do you get them to reach the ceiling?" I asked.

"A stepladder!" she explained.

I didn't know what to say. I definitely had a torch at home, I definitely had a stepladder, but I'd NEVER had two glow-in-the-dark stars!

"Shall we go and start learning about stars?" said Gabby, rolling off her bed and opening her bedroom curtains.

"DEFFO!" I said, grabbing my notebook and pencil case and then tucking my glow-in-the-dark stars safely into my pocket.

That's **the trouble with having two glow-in-the-dark stars in your pocket**. I couldn't stop thinking about them.

When I went back downstairs with

Gabby, I was thinking about them.

When we went into Gabby's mum and dad's office, I was thinking about them.

When we sat down at the computer, I was thinking about them.

Even when Gabby turned the computer on, I couldn't stop thinking about them.

Because secretly all I wanted to do was go straight home, get my torch, grab the stepladder, peel the paper off and stick them to the ceiling in my bedroom.

I didn't tell Gabby, though. Because we had lots of other stars to find out about first.

Well, Gabby did. Because she knows
which buttons to press on a computer.

Finding out about stars was really interesting. Well, it would have been if I hadn't had two glow-in-the-dark stars in my pocket.

Having two glow-in-the-dark stars in my pocket made it really hard for me to listen to anything Gabby was saying.

I did write down the different colours that stars can be, though.

And I wrote down the name of the brightest star in the sky. (No, it isn't Twinkle Twinkle, in case you are wondering.)

But Gabby wrote down most of the rest. Especially all the stuff about constellations.

The trouble with constellations is they are soooooooo confusing!! And sooooooooo difficult to draw!

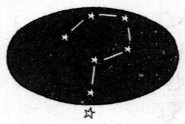

Thank goodness my mum was on time when she came to pick me up.

As soon I got back in the car, I took my glow-in-the-dark stars straight out of my pocket and showed them to my mum.

"That was kind of Gabby," said my mum. "I hope you said thank you."

"I haven't stopped thanking her!"

I smiled. "Will you help me stick them on my ceiling when we get home?"

"Of course I will," Mum said, not realizing how difficult it was going to be!

CHAPTER 9

The trouble with sticking a glow-in-the-dark star to your ceiling is you have to get it in exactly the right place. Especially if you've had the extra-brilliant idea of making the light bulb in your bedroom be the Moon!

Trouble is, my mum had never done glow-in-the-dark stars before, so it made it really hard for me to decide exactly where to stick them.

"Left a bit . . . right a bit . . . back a bit . . .

"Over a bit . . . over a bit more . . . back a bit . . . left a bit . . .

"Sideways to the left . . . sideways to the right . . .

"Too close . . . too wide apart . . . not wide apart enough . . .

"**STICK!**

"Sorry, unstick . . .

"Let's try it over there . . .

"Right a bit . . . right a bit more . . . right a teensy bit more . . . right a squidge . . . left a squodge . . .

"Left a bit more . . . left a bit . . . left a bit . . . back a bit . . . back a bit more . . .

"Right a teensy bit . . . towards me a teensy bit . . . towards you a teensy bit . . .

"**STICK!**

"Sorry, unstick.

"Let's try it over there . . .

"Can we move the Moon?"

"No, we can't move the Moon, Daisy.
The Moon is wired into the ceiling!!"

"OK, left a bit . . . down a bit . . . I
mean, towards you a bit . . . back to me
a bit . . . back to you a weensy bit . . .
back to you a teensy-weensy bit . . .

"Hold it there . . .

"Towards you a nifty-nofty bit . . .

"Back to me a nofty-nifty bit . . .

"**STICK!**

"Perfect!

"Sorry, unstick.

"It might be better over there.

"Or over there . . .

"Or over there . . .

"Or over there . . .

"Or maybe over there . . .

"Actually, can we try it over there?

"Not there . . .

"There . . .

"Perfect . . .

"STICK!"

"It won't stick, Daisy!" puffed Mum.

"Why won't it stick?" I frowned.

"Because I've stuck it and unstuck it so many times, the sticky has completely stopped sticking!" explained Mum.

"Gabby never said anything about

that happening." I frowned. "What are we going to do now?"

"Leave it with me," sighed Mum. "I'll stick it once and for all!

"There . . . STUCK!"

124

The trouble with sticking your SECOND glow-in-the-dark star to your ceiling is it's TWICE as difficult, because the best place has already been taken!!

Poor old Mum. She got into such a tizz, trying to get my second star into the second-best perfect place! I'm guessing when she was my age, it was cloudy all the time.

Luckily, thanks to me, we got there in the end.

When both of my stars were stuck in exactly the right place, they looked AMAZING. Especially after I'd shone my torch over them again.

And pulled my curtains.

And closed my bedroom door.

And lain back down on my bed.

I could just look at them and look at them and look at them.

Without the sticky unsticking either!

Three cheers for superglue!

CHAPTER 10

By the time we'd finished doing my star arranging, it was nearly starting to get dark!!

"I know, Daisy!" said my mum. "How about, instead of us having tea in the kitchen, like we normally do, we have a special stargazers' dinner in the garden instead?"

"A special stargazers' dinner in the garden instead!" I gasped.

"For two." Mum smiled. "Just you, me and a couple of sun loungers."

When I heard Mum was inviting the

sun loungers, I guessed she needed a lie-down. But that was OK. It was still a really exciting idea.

"What if it's cloudy again?" I asked.

"There isn't a cloud in the sky." Mum smiled.

"Can we have mini sausages?" I asked.

"I'll do mini sausages and some cheese-and-ham sandwiches as well," said Mum. "And I'll make a flask of coffee for me, and I'll do a bottle of squash for you."

"Can we have yogurts too?" I asked.

"Yes, we can have yogurts too," said Mum.

"And Crunchy Cream biscuits?"

"If you haven't already eaten them all," she said, smiling.

"There's one left," I said.

While my mum was making our special stargazers' dinner, I got the sun loungers out of the shed.

The trouble with sun loungers is you can put them into different positions.

If you make them really flat, you can lie down and look up at the sky, but your orange squash goes all over you when you try to drink it.

If you sit the back of the sun lounger up, you can sit up to drink your orange squash without spilling it and eat your mini sausages without choking. Trouble is, you don't get a very good view of the sky.

In the end we decided to sit up first and lie flat second.

Lying flat on a sun lounger, looking up at the stars, is one of the best things I've ever done. You should have seen how many stars there were in the sky! I lost count after fifty-three! Mostly because one star kept moving around all over the place.

Mum reckons it wasn't a star at all; it was an aeroplane.

It looked like a star to me.

"Mum, do you know what a constellation is?" I asked. "Gabby and me have been learning about them on her computer."

"I only know *The Plough*," said Mum.

"What's a plough?" I asked.

"It's a machine for digging furrows in farmers' fields," said Mum.

"What's a furrow?" I asked.

"It's a long line in the soil for planting seeds in," said Mum.

It's OK, I knew what seeds were. And soil.

"Where is *The Plough*?" I asked.

"Up there!" said Mum, pointing up at the sky.

The trouble with pointing up there was I had no idea where Mum was pointing.

"Where do you mean?" I asked.

"Up there," said Mum.

"Where?" I asked.

"Up there," she said. "Just follow where my finger is pointing . . .

"See the Moon . . . now right a bit . . . right a bit more . . . right a teensy bit more . . . right a squidge . . . left a squodge . . .

"Right a nifty bit, left a nifty-nofty bit . . .

"Left a bit more . . . left a bit . . . left a bit . . . back a bit . . . back a bit more . . .

"Right a teensy bit . . . towards me a teensy bit . . . towards you a teensy bit . . .

"Now STICK!"

"Very funny." I sighed.

"OK, follow my finger again," laughed my mum. "See the seven bigger stars all grouped together? If you join them like a dot-to-dot, they make the outline of a saucepan. See, a wonky-handled saucepan?"

"SO WHY IS IT CALLED 'THE PLOUGH' IF IT LOOKS LIKE A WONKY-HANDLED SAUCEPAN?" I asked. "WHY ISN'T IT CALLED 'THE WONKY-HANDLED SAUCEPAN'?!"

"Because, Daisy, wonky-handled saucepans weren't invented when constellations were invented," said my mum.

Once I realized that constellations are basically just dot-to-dots in the sky, I started to get the hang of looking for them.

"There are lots to be found if you know where to look," said my mum.

Trouble is, I didn't know where to look. Apart from up.

"If you ask me, constellation stars should have numbers on them," I said. "If they had numbers on them, like proper dot-to-dots, then people could see which way to join them up!"

"I think that's a brilliant idea," said Mum. "We should write to the NASA Space Agency and ask them to do the numbering next time they send a rocket into space. In the meantime, why don't we see if we can discover some new constellations of our own?!"

Believe me, discovering new constellations of your own is a whole lot easier than finding someone else's old ones.

Mum found *The String of Spaghetti*.

I found *The Haribo*.
Mum found *The*

Wiggly Worm,
although I
thought it
looked more
like a broken
rubber band.

By the time I'd
found *The Wonky
Slug* it was time
for bed.

"Race you up
the stairs!" I said, jumping off my sun
lounger, running indoors and throwing
my hoody on the hallway floor. I

couldn't wait to get my pyjamas on; I couldn't wait to wash my face; I couldn't wait to clean my teeth; and I couldn't wait to get into bed!

Because guess what I was going to be gazing at next?!! (Until I fell asleep.)

You've guessed it! MY TWO GLOW-IN-THE-DARK STARS!!

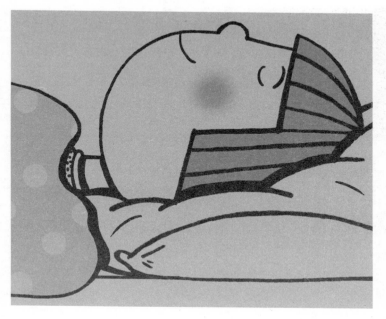

CHAPTER 11

The trouble with Sunday mornings is my mum always wants to have a lie-in.

I only want to have lie-ins on school days, never on Saturdays or Sundays.

Last Sunday, though, I definitely wanted to have a lie-in! In fact, last Sunday I didn't just have a lie-in: I had a lie-in and in and in and in!!!!

Guess what time I got up? HALF PAST

ONE IN THE AFTERNOON! Even then I only got up because my mum told me my eyes would go funny if I kept staring at my glow-in-the-dark stars.

As soon as I had got dressed, I made a phone call to Gabby to tell her about all the actual stargazing I had done with my mum the night before.

Guess what Gabby told me she had found out on the computer? Apparently *The Plough* ISN'T a constellation! It's just a small part of a much bigger constellation called *The Great Bear*.

And double guess what? When you do the dot-to-dots on *The Great Bear,* IT DOESN'T LOOK ANYTHING LIKE A GREAT

BEAR EITHER! It doesn't even look like *A Rubbish Bear* – it looks more like a pointy-nosed lizard.

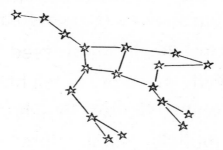

Honestly, whoever named the constellations in olden times must have had the worst telescope in the world.

As soon as I'd finished my lunch, I put my pyjamas on again and went straight back to bed. Because bed is the comfiest place I know to practise drawing stars.

Did you know there is a secret way of drawing stars that makes them perfect every time?

My mum showed me how to do them after she had finished loading the dishwasher.

All you need to draw the perfect star is two triangles!

Draw your first triangle the right way up. And then draw your second triangle on top of it, the other way around!

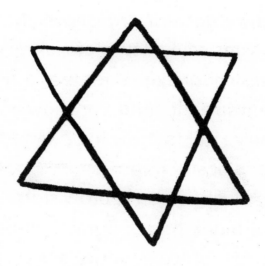

SEE! The perfect star!
What a busy day I'd had!

Being able to draw perfect stars is exactly the right skill you need to have if you are going to do a Team Stars presentation to your class.

If you've got star-drawing skills, you can do skies with a few stars, skies with loads of stars or even skies with a zillion stars – it just depends on how much time you've got to draw them. And how big your piece of paper is.

I had all afternoon to draw stars, plus loads of blank pages in my notebook, plus loads of colouring pens in my pencil case too. By the time I'd finished practising, I was probably the best star drawer the world has ever known.

When I realized it was nearly night-time again, I asked my mum if we could have another stargazing dinner in the garden. But she said no, because I was wearing pyjamas, plus I had school in the morning too.

That's **the trouble with having school in the morning**. It totally stops the evening being any fun at all.

Still, at least I didn't have to get ready for bed after dinner.

I'd been ready for bed nearly all day!

CHAPTER 12

When I woke up on Monday morning, I couldn't get dressed quick enough. In fact, I got dressed so quick, I put my school jumper on back to front!

"It's Space Week, it's Space Week, it's Space Week!" I sang, as I walked into the kitchen for breakfast.

"It's Space Week, it's Space Week, it's Space Week!" I sang, as I left my house to meet Gabby.

"*It's Space Week, it's Space Week, it's Space Week!*" we both sang all the way to school!

When we got into the playground, absolutely everyone in my class was excited about Space Week!

Laura Donnelly had been to the library on Saturday to learn about the Sun and bumped into Sanjay while she was there! Daniel Carrington had got a telescope for his birthday; Chelsea Brent had been to the craft

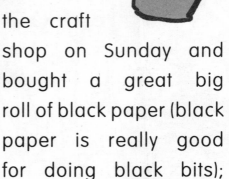

shop on Sunday and bought a great big roll of black paper (black paper is really good for doing black bits);

David Alexander had watched space films all weekend;

Lily Hanrahan had made a rocket out of a washing-up liquid bottle; Collette Simpson had made

a space helmet out of a bucket; and . . . wait for it . . . Jack Beechwhistle had been kidnapped by aliens. At least that's what he told everyone.

According to Jack, he was out on his bike at midnight last Saturday when an alien spaceship came down from space, hovered and then beamed him and his bike up into their spaceship.

"Why did they do that?" asked Paula Potts.

"They wanted my knowledge," said Jack.

"What knowledge?" I asked.

"My survival knowledge," he said. "If you're an alien and you want to take over another planet, then first of all you need to learn how to survive on that planet before your invasion begins. Especially if you want to hide in the woods for a while."

"What survival knowledge do you know?" asked Paula.

"Loads," said Jack. "How to make a den, what tree bark you can eat, how to talk to squirrels, how to camouflage yourself against being seen by humans."

"Did you escape?" asked Paula.

"I'm here now, aren't I?" said Jack.

"How did you escape?" I asked.

"They had me tied up in a chair and were just about to suck my brain out through my ears, when I managed to break free from their ropes," said Jack.

"As soon as I undid their space knots, I jumped back on my bike and cycled out of their spaceship into space."

"Did they chase you?" asked Paula.

"They tried to," said Jack, "but luckily the wheels on my bike are fitted with hyperzoom tyres. No one can catch me when I switch to hyperzoom."

"Do you think they'll be back?" Paula asked.

"Bound to be," said Jack, "but I'll be ready for them."

No one in the playground believed Jack had been kidnapped by aliens. Apart from Paula Potts. Jack is always telling stories about his made-up adventures. Plus if I was an alien, I'd want to suck Barry Morely's knowledge out, not Jack's.

I wouldn't mind getting some of those hyperzoom tyres for my scooter, though.

As soon as the bell for morning lessons went, everyone in 5C rocketed out of the playground and straight into school. Well, we rocketed as far as the corridor. That's when we saw Mr Copford coming towards us. We did sensible walking after that.

When we got into our classroom, Mrs Peters wasn't just sitting on her desk again – she was smiling on her desk again too! Plus behind her was a great big message that she had written on the whiteboard.

"WELCOME
TO
SPACE WEEK!" it read.

As soon as Gabby and I read the message, we went straight over to Mrs Peters and told her we had both decorated our bedroom ceilings with glow-in-the-dark stars!

Mrs Peters told us that Planet Earth has some of the most wonderful ceiling decorations in the Universe and that one day we should go to Italy and visit the ceilings painted by Michael and Angelo. Michael and Angelo were olden-day painter-decorators. Except they didn't do bedrooms; they only did churches.

(Gabby and I have looked them up on her mum and dad's computer. They weren't very good at stars. Or drawing clothes.)

"GOOD MORNING, CHILDREN!!!" said Mrs Peters, once everyone had finally sat down at their desks and stopped chattering. "What is the name of the day today?"

"Monday!!!" everyone shouted.

"And what is the name of the week, this week?"

"SPACE WEEK!" everyone cheered.

"Space Week indeed!" smiled Mrs Peters. "I hope you have all been busy over the weekend, exploring the special space subjects I have asked you to study."

"I have! I have! I have! We have! We have!" everyone shouted together.

"This afternoon Team Sun will be the first team to share their special Sun findings with the class," said Mrs Peters.

"TEAM SUN! TEAM SUN! TEAM SUN!" everybody chanted, until Mrs Peters did her 'silence is golden' action again.

"Team Sun, we are very much looking forward to your class talk!" said Mrs Peters.

"LAURA! DANIEL! LIAM! MELANIE! BERNADETTE!" we all chanted, until Mrs Peters had to not only do her 'silence is golden' action again, but this time do it standing on her chair!

171

"Team Sun, you will have the rest of this morning to work on your presentation. If you would like to use the classroom during lunch break, feel free to do so. The rest of the class, please use every minute of every morning this week to work on your presentations too. Space Week will begin the moment we have returned from morning assembly."

"MORNING ASSEMBLY?" everybody groaned. "Do we still have to go to morning assembly?"

"Yes, you have to go to morning assembly," said Mrs Peters. "The entire school has to go to morning assembly."

172

"But morning assemblies are boring!" everybody groaned.

"Morning assemblies can be very informative," said Mrs Peters. "And joyful."

Thank goodness we only have morning assemblies on Mondays. Because every morning for the rest of last week it was SPACE, SPACE, SPACE all the way!

CHAPTER 13

Space Week was the best week I've ever had at school in my entire life!

We listened to so many amazing space talks . . .!

M O N

DAY

TOGETHER:

"THE SUN HAS GOT HIS HAT ON
HIP-HIP-HIP HOORAY!
WE LOVE THE SUN
WE'VE NOW BEGUN
OUR SUN TALK FOR TODAY!"

Laura: The Sun is very important.

TOGETHER: THAT IS VERY TRUE.

Daniel C.: The Sun gives us sunlight and sunshine and suntans.

TOGETHER: THAT IS VERY NICE.

Liam: It can also give us sunburn if we're not careful.

TOGETHER: THAT IS VERY WORRYING.

Melanie: Without the Sun, nothing would grow except darkness and cold.

TOGETHER: THAT IS VERY SAD.

Bernadette: Did you know that the Sun is about five billion years old?

TOGETHER: THAT IS VERY OLD!

Laura: Did you know the Sun is actually a burning ball of mostly hydrogen gas?

TOGETHER: THAT IS VERY AMAZING!

Daniel C.: Did you know that the Sun is actually a star?

TOGETHER: THAT IS VERY SURPRISING!

Liam: Did you know that the Sun is fifteen million degrees hot in the middle?

TOGETHER: THAT IS VERY HOT!

Melanie: Did you know that you could fit a million Planet Earths inside the Sun? Well, you could, but your fingers would get burned doing it!

TOGETHER: THAT IS VERY BIG!

Bernadette: Did you know the Sun is so big it takes 100,000 years for the heat in the middle to reach its surface?

TOGETHER: THAT IS UNBELIEVABLE!

Laura: Planet Earth takes 365 and a quarter days to spin once round the Sun.

TOGETHER: THAT IS CALLED AN ORBIT.

Daniel C.: Sometimes we can't see the Sun because the Moon gets in the way.

TOGETHER: THAT IS CALLED A SOLAR ECLIPSE.

Liam: Sometimes when the Sun is too hot, children are forced to beg . . .

Melanie: And beg . . .

Bernadette: And beg . . .

Laura: And beg for the ONLY thing on Planet Earth that can keep them alive.

TOGETHER: THAT IS CALLED AN ICE CREAM! WE HOPE YOU ENJOYED OUR TALK!

TUES

DAY

Nishta: The Moon comes out at night.

Harry: The Moon is the brightest thing in our night sky.

Vicky: If the Moon didn't come out at night, foxes, badgers, hedgehogs and other night-time animals wouldn't be able to see where they were going.

Colin: The Moon has been orbiting Planet Earth for 4.3 billion years.

Daniel M.: Things in the universe that spin round planets are called satellites.

TOGETHER: THIS MEANS THE MOON IS A SATELLITE OF PLANET EARTH.

Nishta: The Moon is made of hard rock.

TOGETHER: NOT HARD CHEESE!

Harry: The Moon circles Planet Earth twelve times a year.

Vicky: That is why one Earth year is divided into twelve months.

Colin: The Moon is 384,400 kilometres away from Planet Earth.

TOGETHER: THAT IS WHY YOU CAN'T CATCH A BUS TO GET THERE!!!!!

Daniel M.: In 1969, humans landed on the Moon for the first time in a spacecraft called Apollo 11.

Nishta: There were three astronauts in the rocket.

Harry: Two years later, an Apollo 14 astronaut even played golf on the Moon's surface!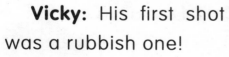

Vicky: His first shot was a rubbish one!

TOGETHER: HIS SECOND SHOT WENT FOR MILES AND MILES AND MILES!!!!!!!!!!!!!!!!!!!!

Colin: If Team Moon built a rocket and took off from our school playground, it would  take us three days to arrive on the Moon.

TOGETHER: WE WOULDN'T PLAY GOLF WHEN WE GOT THERE, THOUGH!

Daniel M.: I'd play cricket.

Nishta: I'd play football!

Harry: I'd play Frisbee!

Vicky: I'd play rounders!

Daniel M.: I'd play tennis!

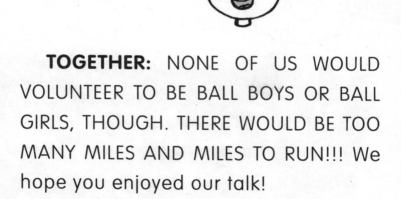

TOGETHER: NONE OF US WOULD VOLUNTEER TO BE BALL BOYS OR BALL GIRLS, THOUGH. THERE WOULD BE TOO MANY MILES AND MILES TO RUN!!! We hope you enjoyed our talk!

W E D N

ESDAY

(TEAM STARS DAY!)

Gabby: Give us an S!

CLASS 5C: S!!!

Me: Give us a T!

CLASS 5C: T!!!

Oliver: Give us an A!

CLASS 5C: A!!!

Paula: Give us an A . . . I mean, an R!

CLASS 5C: R!!!

Sanjay: Give us another S!

CLASS 5C: S!!!

TOGETHER: WHAT HAVE WE GOT???

CLASS 5C: STARS!!!!!

Gabby: Stars light up the sky at night.

Me: Unless it's cloudy.

Oliver: But how we wonder what they are.

Sanjay: There are billions of stars in the night sky.

Paula: All of them,  like the Sun, are made of burning-hot gas.

Gabby: Some stars are  close to Planet Earth.

Me: Some stars are a long way away.

Oliver: But how we wonder what they are.

Gabby: Scientists organize stars by colour and size.

Sanjay: The normal colour for stars is white.

Paula: The hottest stars look bluey-white.

Gabby: The furthest-away stars glow red.

Me: Most of the red ones are really aeroplanes.

Oliver: But how we wonder what they are.

Sanjay: Some stars join up to make constellations.

Paula: Most constellations leave you wondering what they are even once you've joined them up.

Gabby: This one is supposed to be a crab.

Me: This one is supposed to be a lion.

Sanjay: And this one is supposed to be a dog!

Paula: The brightest star is called Polaris.

Gabby: Most people call it  the North Star.

Me: Polar bears look up at the North Star all the time because it is directly above the North Pole.

Sanjay: So do Arctic foxes, Arctic hares, ringed seals and walruses.

Me: But not penguins, because they live at the  South Pole.

Oliver: But how we wonder what they are.

Me: Not yet, Oliver. Everyone knows what penguins are.

Oliver: Sorry.

Sanjay: The fastest stars in the sky are called shooting stars.

Oliver: But how we wonder what they are.

Paula: And if you're wondering what shooting stars are, then you are right to wonder.

TOGETHER: BECAUSE SHOOTING STARS AREN'T STARS AT ALL!

199

Gabby: To be a proper star you have to be made of gas.

Sanjay: Shooting stars are made of rocks.

Gabby: Shooting stars are falling rocks that burst into flames the moment they enter the Earth's atmosphere.

Oliver: But how we wonder what they are.

Me: You've done it again, Oliver.

Oliver: I mean, how we wonder how to draw them.

Me: Thank you, Oliver. Now, if you want to learn the best way to draw a shooting star, or any

kind of star, then the best thing is to

 learn how to draw a normal one first.

This is the best way to draw a normal star.

You can turn your normal star into a shooting star by doing this.

 You can turn your normal star into a bright star by doing this.

You can turn your bright star into a bright blue star by colouring it blue.

Or you can turn your normal star into a far-away star by colouring it red.

 Or if you want to turn it into an aeroplane, add another bit of red and draw some wings on it.

Paula: Movie stars aren't proper stars either, by the way. Neither are pop stars. Because movie stars and pop stars are made of people.

Me: I think people know that, Paula.

Gabby: COME ON, 5C, ALL TOGETHER NOW! GIVE US A TWINKLE, TWINKLE!

CLASS 5C: TWINKLE, TWINKLE!!!!

Sanjay: GIVE US A LITTLE STARS!

Class 5C: LITTLE STARS!!!!

TOGETHER: BECAUSE NOW YOU ALL KNOW WHAT THEY ARE!!!

Me: And how to draw them too!

THUR

Chelsea: What makes things fall to the ground?

TOGETHER: GRAVITY!

Collette: What makes astronauts float in space?

TOGETHER: GRAVITY!

Richard: What makes paddling at the seaside shallow or deep?

TOGETHER: GRAVITY!

Stephanie: What can give something the size of a ladybird the power to crunch something the size of a mountain?

TOGETHER: GRAVITY!

Chelsea: Over to Barry.

Barry: Gravity is an invisible force that pulls objects down to Earth. It isn't a magnetic force because magnets only work on metal.

Collette: Gravity works on tangerines.

Richard: Gravity works on drinks bottles.

Stephanie: Gravity works on tennis balls.

Chelsea: Gravity works on pencil cases.

Barry: Gravity works on the oceans.

TOGETHER: GRAVITY WORKS ON EVERYTHING! INCLUDING HUMANS TOO!

Barry: The higher humans travel into space, the weaker the pull of gravity becomes. The weaker the pull of gravity becomes, the lighter astronauts feel.

Chelsea: Did you know that when astronauts get to the Moon they feel six times lighter? That is why astronauts on the Moon can float and jump such a long way.

Collette: On Planet Earth, the high-jump record is 2.45 metres.

Richard: On the Moon, it would be nearly 15!

Stephanie: On Planet Earth, the long-jump record is nearly 8 metres.

Richard: On the Moon, it would be nearly 48!

Barry: The pull of gravity works in different ways depending on where you are in the universe. But there is one place in space where the pulling force of gravity is so strong that no astronaut or spaceship should EVER, EVER go there.

TOGETHER: DANGER! DANGER!

Barry: That place is called a black hole! Black holes are the most dangerous and destructive places in the  whole universe. They are like the mouths of hungry space monsters, with lips that suck like Hoovers and teeth that crunch like dinosaurs. Even a black hole the size of a pinhead has the pulling power to swallow a mountain. Supermassive black holes could pull and munch and crunch and swallow as many as a million Suns! And then still be hungry for more.

It's like going to the school canteen at lunchtime . . .

   eating your sandwiches,

   then eating your lunchbox,

   then eating the table,

   then eating the dinner ladies,

   then eating all your friends,

   then eating your entire school,

   then eating the town that you live in,

   and then still feeling hungry after you've burped!

TOGETHER: ON EARTH, GRAVITY IS OUR FRIEND.

Barry: But in space, gravity can be our friend or . . .

TOGETHER: OUR DEADLY ENEMY!

Barry: So please, if you ever grow up to be an astronaut and you see a black hole coming . . .

TOGETHER: DROP EVERYTHING AND RUN! We hope you liked our talk!

F R I

DAY

Lily: There are eight planets in our solar system.

Jack: Only one of them has ice-cream vans, sweet shops and toy shops.

Lottie: All of them circle round the Sun.

Dottie: If you want to be a proper planet, you HAVE to circle round a sun.

David: If you look like a proper planet but you circle round a planet, then you can ONLY be a moon.

TOGETHER: SORRY, TEAM MOON!

Lily: The four closest planets to the Sun are Mercury, then Venus, then Earth, then Mars.

Jack: All of these planets are in the inner solar system and are made of metals and rocks.

Lottie: The four planets furthest from the Sun are Jupiter, then Saturn, then Uranus, then Neptune.

Dottie: All of these planets are in the outer solar system and are mostly made of gases.

TOGETHER: HANDS UP IF YOU CAN REMEMBER THE CLOSEST PLANET TO THE SUN!

HANDS UP IF YOU CAN REMEMBER THE FOURTH-CLOSEST PLANET TO THE SUN!

HANDS UP IF YOU CAN REMEMBER THE SEVENTH-CLOSEST PLANET TO THE SUN!

David: We couldn't either until Jack helped us!

Jack: If you need to remember which eight planets are closest to the Sun, and you want to get them in the right order, remember my eight-word sentence!

223

Think **ME**
think **ME**rcury,
think **V**
think **V**enus,
think **E**
think **E**arth,
think **MA**
think **MA**rs,

think **JU**
think **JU**piter,
think **S**
think **S**aturn,
think **U**
think **U**ranus,
think **N**
think **N**eptune.

See! All eight planets, all in the right order. And if Pluto is ever allowed to be a planet again, add **P**istachios to the sentence in brackets at the end.

Think **P**,
think **P**luto!

Lily: Every planet in our solar system is different.

Jack: Mercury is the smallest and hottest because it is closest to the Sun. If you bought an ice cream on Mercury, the ice cream would melt in a nanosecond and your cone would burst into flames. Then so would you.

Lottie: Venus is similar in size to Earth but it's as dry as a hundred deserts. If you bought an ice cream there, you'd drown in sweat before you could pay for it, plus your throat would be so dry you wouldn't be able to say which ice cream you wanted.

Dottie: Earth is the best planet of all, except none of the other planets give you homework.

David: Mars wasn't named after a chocolate bar; a chocolate bar was named after Mars. Some people call Mars 'the Red Planet' instead. Which isn't a good name for a chocolate bar at all.

Lily: Jupiter is the biggest planet in our solar system. It is two and a half times bigger than all the other planets put together. If aliens existed on Jupiter, then they would have very squeaky voices, because one of the gases Jupiter is made of is helium.

Jack: Saturn is known as 'the Ringed Planet' because it has non-stop rings of rocks spinning round it. If aliens opened a theme park, Saturn would be it, except the rocks would be quite uncomfortable to sit on.

Lottie: Uranus is super cold and would be the best place for aliens to keep their ice creams.

Dottie: Neptune is the windiest planet in the solar system and the perfect place for aliens to fly kites. As long as they didn't fly them too close to the Sun.

TOGETHER: IF WE COULD INVENT A PLANET, WE WOULD CALL IT

PLANET HAPPEA!!

David: Planet Happea would be the greenest planet in the universe.

Lily: It would be kind to animals.

Jack: Kind to trees.

Lottie: Kind to birds.

Dottie: And insects too.

David: It would have Christmas all year round!

CLASS 5C: YAYYY!!!

Lily: Children would be allowed to have a birthday every month!

CLASS 5C: YAYYY!!!

Jack: Toys would be free!

CLASS 5C: YAYYY!

Lottie: Sweets would be free!

CLASS 5C: YAYYY!!!

Dottie: Ice creams would be free!

CLASS 5C: YAYYY!!!

David: Homework would be banned!

CLASS 5C: YAYYY!!!

Lily: And schools would only be allowed to teach lessons about SPACE!

TOGETHER: WE HOPE YOU ENJOYED OUR TALK!

CHAPTER 14

At the very beginning of Space Week, Gabby and me thought our talk was definitely going to be the best, but by the end of Space Week we thought everyone's talks were the best! (Apart from the way they drew stars.)

Mrs Peters thought Jack's sentence for remembering the planets was 'a bit indelicate', which I think means 'not very suitable for children'. (Because it's got someone being sick in it.) She even suggested we come up with some different sentences of our own. "**M**y **V**elvet **E**lephant" is as far as I could get, though. Plus I liked Jack's sentence best. So did everyone else in class, so we're going to remember his sentence instead.

All through the five days of Space Week

it had been space, space, space, space and more space, with no space for anything else in between! Everyone had talked about space in class, everyone had talked about space in the playground and we had even talked about space on the way home from school!

Even when the teams had finished doing their space presentations, they were still borrowing space books from the library. In fact, our school library completely ran out of space books to lend! And books about healthy eating. (Some people didn't know the difference between lettuce-type rocket and space-type rocket.)

On Tuesday, during lunch break, Jack Beechwhistle had also taught everyone in the playground how to speak Venus language. (That's the planet that he was kidnapped to. Or says he was.)

"If kidnappers from Venus have taught you how to speak Venus language, then prove it!" said Gabby.

"This is what they said to me when they tied me up," Jack said back.

"Vello, Vack Veechwhistle. Ve var valiens vrom Venus. Vive vus vour vnowledge."

According to Jack, that's how aliens from Venus speak. They start all of their words, I mean 'vords', with a V.

237

On Wednesday in the playground the girls had played the boys at Space Football. Space Football is the same as normal football, only the girls were Angels FC and the boys were Aliens United. Angels FC beat Aliens United seventeen–nil because the boys lost the toss, which meant they had to be aliens with one leg. (It's really hard to hop and score goals at the same time.)

If you're wondering what Angels FC would have had to do if they'd lost the toss, they'd all have had to play on one wing!

On Thursday Lottie and Dottie had secretly asked Mrs Peters if they could do a special presentation of their own, but once Mrs Peters had heard what it was about, she had said no.

So they did their presentation at breaktime on the hopscotch squares instead.

Guess what eight terrible things would happen to you if you forgot to put your spacesuit on in space! Close your eyes if you don't want to know!

Number 1: You'd immediately run out of breath! Because in outer space there's no air to breathe!

Number 2: You'd poo yourself!

Number 3: Your blood would boil!

Number 4: Your veins would clog up!

Number 5: Your whole body would blow up like a balloon!

Number 6: You'd get instant sunburn! (With no cream to put on it because you left your suncream in your spaceship.)

Number 7: You'd get blasted by gamma rays from the stars AND the Sun at the same time!

Number 8: And freeze-blasted by temperatures a hundred times colder than the North Pole and South Pole put together!

That's the bad news. The good news is if you were rescued by a space ambulance within sixty seconds you might actually survive!

Everyone who listened to Lottie and Dottie's presentation has been put off being an astronaut for life. Apart from

241

Jack Beechwhistle. Jack says with hyperzoom tyres he can handle anything space has to throw at him. Including comets and meteors.

He even said if he was hungry enough he would eat a black hole.

It was still really sad when we got to the end of Friday, though. It's the only time I've ever, ever, ever wanted school to stay open at the weekend!

When the bell went at the end of the day yesterday, Gabby and me decided to keep Space Week going by seeing if we could speak Venus language all the way home.

<u>WITHOUT LAUGHING!</u>

"Vit's va vig vity Vpace Veek vis vover, visn't vit, Vaisy?"

"Ves, Vabby, vit's va very vig vi . . . !!!!!"

We didn't get very far.

I mean 'var'!!!!!

CHAPTER 15

The trouble with Space Week being over was not only was it a very big pity, it meant I had nothing to do. Apart from lie on my bed and look at the stars Gabby had given me.

Even if I looked at them the other way round it felt like I had nothing to do.

Mum thought of loads of things I could do. She said I could tidy my room,

hoover the lounge, peel some potatoes,
cook the tea, do the food shopping, cut
the grass, weed the flower beds, empty

245

the dishwasher, do the ironing, tidy the shed, clean the car and wallpaper the lounge.

How lazy can a mum get???!!!!

Luckily, when I was lying on my bed looking at my stars I had the most brilliant idea in the universe. It wasn't just brilliant either; it was SPACETASTIC! In fact, it was SOOOOOOOOOOOOO SPACETASTIC, I jumped off my bed, ran

down the stairs and rang Gabby straight away!

"What are you doing tomorrow morning?" I gasped.

"Going shopping again with my mum," she said. "I always go shopping with my mum on Saturdays."

"Can you get out of it?" I asked.

"Not really," she said.

"Then as soon as you get home, grab your pencil case and all your colouring things and come round to my house straight away!"

"Why, what are we going to do?" Gabby asked.

"I'll tell you what we're going to do," I said. "WE'RE GOING TO TAKE MY BEDROOM CEILING TO NEW HEIGHTS!"

CHAPTER 16

The trouble with taking my bedroom ceiling to new heights is I probably should have asked my mum first.

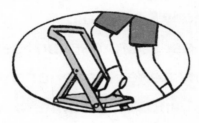

I was sure she would have said yes, only she was busy doing some of the jobs she had been too lazy to do the day before. So I didn't want to bother her.

Not because I'd had a bad idea or

anything, but because if mums are on their hands and knees, busy washing the kitchen floor, or crawling under the car to look for rusty bits, or maybe doing some low-down dusting, it can be really hard for them to understand what new heights actually are.

The trouble with not bothering her is she got really bothered when she saw what Gabby and I had done to my bedroom ceiling.

This is how Michael and Angelo decorated their ceiling in Italy:

Photo copyright © agcreativelab - stock.adobe.com

This is how Gabby and me decorated the ceiling in my bedroom:

The trouble with doing stars on your ceiling with felt-tip is felt-tip doesn't wash off.

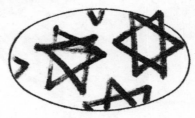

The trouble with doing black holes in Magic Marker is Magic Marker doesn't wash off either. And if you paint over it, the black holes keep showing through.

The trouble with doing pink holes, green holes, blue holes and other coloured holes is you need far more felt-tips and Magic Markers than just black ones.

The trouble with using biros on your ceiling is biros don't work upside down. Unless you really dig in.

The trouble with digging in is it makes scratches on the ceiling.

The trouble with doing shooting stars in glitter glue is glitter glue drips on bedspreads.

WHICH IS GRAVITY'S FAULT, NOT MINE!

"Grounded!" said Mum, taking the stepladders out of my bedroom. "Grounded, grounded, grounded, grounded," I heard her saying all the way down the stairs.

As soon as Gabby got back to her house, she called me to see how long I'd been grounded for.

My mum still hasn't calmed down yet, so at the moment it's still a billion years.

Oh well, at least my two glow-in-the-dark stars are still stuck to the ceiling.

THREE HUNDRED CHEERS FOR SUPERGLUE!!!!!!!!!!!!!!!!!!!!!

P.S. Here's some more space jokes I heard on the playground!

Q. What do aliens use to stop their trousers from falling down?
A. An asteroid belt.

Q. How do you get a baby astronaut to sleep?
A. You rocket!

Q. What do you call a spaceship with water dripping from it?
A. A crying saucer!

Q. Where do space cows live?
A. The Moooooooooon!

Q. What do you call an alien with six eyes?
A. An aliiiiiien!

Q. Why did the Sun go to school ?
A. To get brighter!

Q. What happened to that golf ball that went miles and miles and miles?
A. It got a black hole in one!

I made that one up myself!
   Well, Bernadette Laine did.

I can't be good at everything!

DAISY'S
TROUBLE INDEX

The trouble with . . .

More than a million

DAISY

books sold!

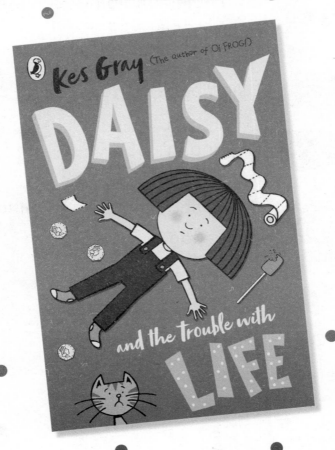

Kes Gray (The author of Oi FROG!)

DAISY

and the trouble with

ZOOS

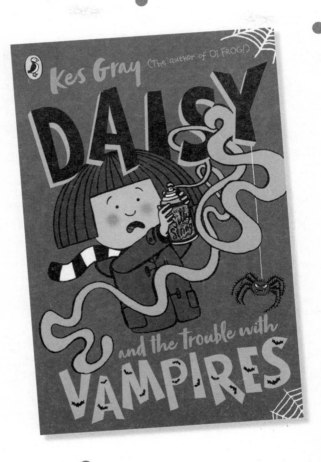

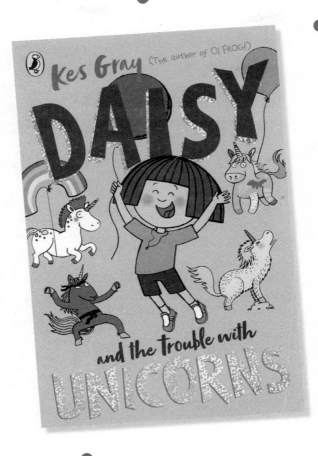

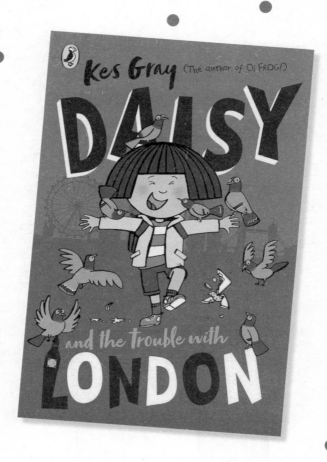